DEAR MOUSE FRIENDS, WELCOME TO THE

STONE AGE!

WELCOME TO THE STONE AGE . . . AND THE WORLD OF THE CAVEMICE!

CAPITAL: OLD MOUSE CITY

POPULATION: WE'RE NOT SURE. (MATH DOESN'T EXIST YET!) BUT BESIDES CAVEMICE, THERE ARE PLENTY OF DINOSAURS, <u>WAY</u> TOO MANY SABER-TOOTHED TIGERS, AND FEROCIOUS CAVE BEARS — BUT NO MOUSE HAS EVER HAD THE COURAGE TO COUNT THEM!

TYPICAL FOOD: PETRIFIED CHEESE SOUP

NATIONAL HOLIDAY: GREAT ZAP DAY, WHICH CELEBRATES THE DISCOVERY OF FIRE. RODENTS EXCHANGE GRILLED CHEESE SANDWICHES ON THIS HOLIDAY.

NATIONAL DRINK: MAMMOTH MILKSHAKES

CLIMATE: Unpredictable, WITH FREQUENT METEOR SHOWERS

cheese soup

milkshake

MONEY

SEASHELLS OF ALL SHAPES AND SIZES

MEASUREMENT

THE BASIC UNIT OF MEASUREMENT IS BASED ON THE LENGTH OF THE TAIL OF THE LEADER OF THE VILLAGE. A UNIT CAN BE DIVIDED INTO A HALF TAIL OR QUARTER TAIL. THE LEADER IS ALWAYS READY TO PRESENT HIS TAIL WHEN THERE IS A DISPUTE.

THE CAVEMICE

Geronimo

Trap

Thea

Benjamin

Bugsy Wugsy

Hercule Poirat

Grandma Ratrock

Geronimo Stilton

CAVEMICE

DON'T WAKE THE DINOSAUR!

Scholastic Inc.

ISBN 978-0-545-65603-0

Text by Geronimo Stilton
Original title *Dinosauro che dorme non piglia topi!*
Cover by Flavio Ferron
Illustrations by Giuseppe Facciotto (design) and Daniele Verzini (color)
Graphics by Marta Lorini and Chiara Cebraro

Special thanks to Tracey West
Translated by Lidia Morson Tramontozzi
Interior design by Becky James

12 11 10 9 8 7 6 5 4 3 2 1   14 15 16 17 18 19/0

Printed in the U.S.A.   40
First printing, November 2014

MANY AGES AGO, ON PREHISTORIC MOUSE ISLAND, THERE
WAS A VILLAGE CALLED OLD MOUSE CITY. IT WAS INHABITED
BY BRAVE *RODENT SAPIENS* KNOWN AS THE CAVEMICE.
DANGERS SURROUNDED THE MICE AT EVERY TURN:
EARTHQUAKES, METEOR SHOWERS, FEROCIOUS DINOSAURS,
AND FIERCE GANGS OF SABER-TOOTHED TIGERS. BUT THE
BRAVE CAVEMICE FACED IT ALL WITH A SENSE OF HUMOR,
AND WERE ALWAYS READY TO LEND A HAND TO OTHERS.
HOW DO I KNOW THIS? I DISCOVERED AN
ANCIENT BOOK WRITTEN BY MY ANCESTOR, GERONIMO
STILTONOOT! HE CARVED HIS STORIES INTO STONE TABLETS
AND ILLUSTRATED THEM WITH HIS ETCHINGS.
I AM PROUD TO SHARE THESE STONE AGE STORIES WITH
YOU. THE EXCITING ADVENTURES OF THE CAVEMICE WILL
MAKE YOUR FUR STAND ON END, AND THE JOKES WILL
TICKLE YOUR WHISKERS! HAPPY READING!

Geronimo Stilton

WARNING! DON'T IMITATE THE CAVEMICE.
WE'RE NOT IN THE STONE AGE ANYMORE!

BOSS, CAN YOU HEAR ME?

If I say "spring," what do you think of? SUN? Flowers? Little baby **pterodactyls** happily chirping in their nests? Well, it was spring in *Old Mouse City* — but there was nothing springlike about it. To start with, it was **freezing** cold!

There was a brisk north wind **blowing** that chilled me down to my bones. Dark, gloomy ☁☁☁☁☁☁ filled with rain hovered in the sky from morning till night. Every few hours, the clouds would unleash sudden ᴛᴏʀʀᴇɴᴛɪᴀʟ showers that crashed down with prehistoric power.

It was so cold that my cheese was turning into cheesicles. In other words, it was a truly **CH-CH-CHILLING** spring!

But luckily for me, I stayed **warm** because I was in my office all the time.

Oops! You might not know me! My name is **GERONIMO STILTONOOT**. I'm the editor

of *The Stone Gazette*, the most famouse prehistoric newspaper (probably because it's the only one!). Each issue has to be chiseled out of stone.

In fact, I was so busy **CHISELING** a stone slab that I didn't notice my assistant, Wiley Upsnoot, who had planted himself behind me.

He made sure I noticed him when he lifted up my earmuffs and shouted in my ear with all his might, "**HEY, BOSS! CAN YOU HEAR ME?**"

Squeak! He scared me so much that I let go of my hammer. It **FLEW** up and then dropped down onto my skull . . .

BONK!

"Are you trying to make me extinct before my time?" I asked.

Wiley smiled, embarrassed.

"Hmm, well, boss . . ."

"Don't call me **BOSS**!" I said.

"Okay, boss."

?! ?! ?!

"**SPIT IT OUT! WHAT IS IT?**"

"Well, it's about the big *Cavemouse Idol* competition tonight, boss . . .

GREGORY GRUNT

I mean, sir . . . I mean, Geronimo!" Wiley said. "The whole village is talking about it."

Of course! **CAVEMOUSE IDOL!** It was organized by a rather unpleasant

6

rodent named Gregory Grunt.

The reason I called him "unpleasant" is because he had never *laughed* in his life. That's why Gregory started the contest — to see if someone, anyone, could make him *laugh*! He had put up a very valuable prize: a STONE CUP sculpted by the famouse prehistoric artist, Leonardo da Fossil. It was so valuable that Gregory had a huge DINOSAUR guarding it!

"Everyone is most excited to see the act by the STENCH BROTHERS," Wiley continued. "Can you believe it, boss? They've only been here a couple of hours and all of Old Mouse City is already *buzzing*!"

7

HOLEY CHEESE! WHAT A MOUSETASTIC PIECE OF NEWS!

Rumor had it that the Stench Brothers were some of the funniest **COMEDY STARS** in the prehistoric world. And here they were in my village! I couldn't pass up this chance to interview them.

I left my cozy office and, struggling against the powerful north wind, I made my way to the STENCH BROTHERS' traveling wagon.

WOOOOOSH! WOOOOOSH!

AAA-CHOO!

Pounded by the gusts of **ICY** wind, I finally got to Singing Rock Square. My poor fur was **frozen**!

I looked around for the Stench Brothers' traveling wagon. I expected to see something **big and fancy**. Instead, I found a wagon that was **RICKETY** and broken-down. Hmm. Was this actually the transportation used by two famouse comedy stars?

As I pondered this, two large, *curly-haired* rodents popped out of the wagon.

Aaa-choo!

"AAA-CHOO!" I announced myself.

9

"Nice to meet you," I said, WIPING my snout. "My name is Geronimo Stiltonoot and I'd like to interview you."

The brothers were twins. One of them raised an eyebrow at me. "Look, Stinky, it's a fan," he sneered. "He wants to —"

"Who knew, Stanky," interrupted the other one. "Even the BONEHEADS in this primitive town are fans of ours!"

"*You're* the primitive mice," I wanted to say — but I didn't want to blow my chance at an interview.

"Actually, I'm a reporter," I explained.

Stinky

Stanky

THE STENCH BROTHERS

"I'd like to give you two an entire slab in *The Stone Gazette.* It's the most famouse newspaper in prehistory!"

The **twins** did a double take.

"A reporter?" said Stinky. "Then perhaps we can give you a teensy-weensy interview, Mr. **Stiltonutt**."

"It's Stilto*noot*," I corrected him. "But . . . **AAA-CHOO!** Could we please go inside the wagon? The wind out here is cold enough to freeze melted cheese!"

"Don't even think of it, **Stiltonoodle**," said Stanky. "The wagon is off-limits. We keep all our tricks of the trade in there. Our equipment, our makeup . . ."

"Actually, my name is Stilto*noot*," I corrected him. "And that's fine. We'll stay outside."

I'll do anything for an interview! With a

shivering paw, I began to chisel my notes on a tiny slab. "Okay, let's begin. Where do you come from? What **routine** will you perform tonight? Do you think you'll win?"

Stinky Stench shook his head. "Whoa! Slow down, **Stiltonose**. First tell us about this tiny little village called Old Mouse City. And then tell us more about this priceless prize cup made by **LEONARDO DA FOSSIL**."

I was getting impatient with them. "Actually . . . **AAA-CHOO!** My name is Stilto*noot*! S-T-I-L-T-O-N-O-O-T!"

"Mr. S-T-I-L-T-O-N-O-I-S-E. Are you going to talk about that PRICELESS cup or not?" Stinky asked.

I sighed. It looked like this interview wasn't going to go my way. The Stench Brothers asked me lots of **QUESTIONS**.

But whenever I asked *them* a question, they changed the subject.

What a primordial mess!

After I had told the twins everything they wanted, Stinky rubbed his paws together.

"Very well, Mr. **STILTONELLY**, we're done. We don't have any more time for you!" he said.

"Yes, run along, Mr. **STILTONEEDLE**," said Stanky.

I turned to leave — and knocked over a bucket behind me. It FLEW up and splashed water all over me! The icy water drenched me from the tips of my ears to the tip of my tail.

Heeeelp!

SPLASH

"**AAA-CHOO!**" I sneezed.

"Looks like your cold is getting worse, **Stiltonerd**," said Stinky.

He was right. My forehead was burning hotter than a pot of cheddar fondue!

BONES AND STONES! NOW I HAD A FEVER!

Depressed, I stumbled back to my office. I couldn't shake the feeling that the Stench Brothers were laughing behind my back. . . .

POOR ME!

I must have **sneezed** a thousand times on the way to the office. I quickly found my assistant, Wiley, and told him about the Stench Brothers.

"Holey cheese, boss!" he cried. "Maybe they can write up their interview with *you* and we can publish that."

"Berry funny," I said through my stuffed-up snout. **"AAA-CHOO!** I'm going to my ca*b*e to rest u*b* a little. Since there's no inter*b*iew, you can re*b*ort on the talent show tonight."

Wiley was **OVERJOYED.**

"Cool, boss! You can count on me."

He **eagerly** picked up a bunch of small slabs so he could take notes and **RUSHED** out of the office.

Cavemouse Idol was about to begin. Every rodent in Old Mouse City tried to *sneak* out of work early to rush to the **SQUARE** and get the best seat. Every rodent but me, that is. I had a raging cold, so I had no choice. I had to miss the show and return to my **CAVE** to rest.

POOR ME! I was in such bad shape. My snout **DRIPPED** like a faucet. My sneezes were louder than a screeching pterodactyl. My throat burned like **lava**. And my head pounded like it had been run over by a herd of **stampeding** Megalosauruses.

I feel awful!

As soon as I got home, I took off my wet green **fur** coat and hung it outside to dry. I put on my **thickest** pajamas (made of mammoth wool) to warm up my fur and put an **ice pack** on my head to help my fever. Then I sank under the blankets in my bed.

Through my **BLAZING** fever I heard the distant cheers and **laughter** of everyone watching the talent show. Depressed, I **sighed** in envy. It sounded as if everybody in the audience of *Cavemouse Idol* was having **FUN**!

Well, I wasn't having any fun at all.

Despite my ice pack, I still felt as **HOT** as a grilled cheese sandwich. I quickly fell into a **deep**, **deep** sleep. . . .

ZZZZZZZZZZ . . .

ZZZZZZZZZZ . . .

ZZZZZZZZZZ . . .

I woke up the following morning filled with energy. My fever was gone and my head felt lighter. My throat didn't sting anymore and my snout had stopped RUNNING. I looked out the window: The pterodactyls were chirping and the sun was shining brightly.

The frcezing-cold north wind had stopped blowing, too.

What a fabumouse morning!

I ate breakfast quickly. I couldn't wait to hear all about the *Cavemouse Idol* contest. But as soon as I stepped out the door, a loud shriek shook my body.

"VARIETY SHOW CONTEST CALLED OFF DUE TO THEFT!"

What? A theft? Then the next shriek shook me.

"THE THIEF GOT PAST THE SLEEPING DINOSAUR GUARD!"

Did that mean . . . ?

"THE DA FOSSIL CUP HAS BEEN STOLEN!"

The shrieking dinosaur

Contest called off!

23

was a news announcer from Gossip Radio, the radio station run by Sally Rockmousen.

I stood there, stunned, as Wiley ran up.

Puff, puff! He caught his breath. "**Big news**, boss!"

"Was the cup really stolen?" I asked.

He nodded. "The thief managed to get past the DINOSAUR guarding it — he was asleep. But that's not all. When the cup vanished, everyone in the city was at the competition. Everyone but *you*, boss."

What was he getting at? I was starting to get a **bAd** feeling when the announcer shrieked again.

"THE THIEF HAS BEEN FOUND!"

GREAT ROCKY BOULDERS! Had Sally's news team already figured out the thief? What a **scoop**! I hated to admit it, but it looked like Gossip Radio had beaten *The Stone Gazette* on this one.

My neighbors quieted down as we all waited to hear who the thief was.

"TWO WITNESSES SAW HIM GET AWAY WITH THE LOOT!" the announcer shrieked.

That sounded convincing.

"AND THE THIEF IS . . ."

The announcer paused, leaving us all in suspense. We all wondered: What kind of a *slimy*, *stinky* snake would do such a thing? That thief was going to be the most unpopular rodent in the city.

"The thief is . . . **Geronimo Stiltonoot**!"

Stunned, I became as petrified as a fossil.

HUUUUUUUUUUUHHHHH?!?!?!

Everyone's eyes turned to me. But . . . but . . .

Bones and stones! What was going on?

After being in shock for a second (well, at least ten seconds), I shook myself out of my **daze**.

I took a deep breath. I knew I wasn't the thief. Once

Can you believe it?

There he is!

I explained my innocence, everyone would understand.

But my fellow citizens didn't give me a chance to squeak. They opened their windows and hurled insults at me.

"Booo! Shame on you!"

Then someone threw a rotten chickenosaurus egg at me!

Then they started throwing vegetables at me! Prehistoric tomatoes, Paleolithic peppers, and Jurassic pumpkins came flying my way.

Boooo!

Hooooot!

Shame on you!

But...

I quickly ran to the office of *The Stone Gazette*, closed the door, and finally breathed a sigh of relief. . . .

Whew!

IT'S A JOKE, RIGHT?

Safe inside the office, I started to think. That accusation had to be a joke, right? And if it was a joke, shouldn't I be laughing?

I was very confused. Then Wiley ran up to me, looking ALARMED.

"Boss! There are a few people waiting outside to see you, boss," he said.

"Wiley, I told you a thousand times not to call me b —"

I STOPPED SUDDENLY.

A parade of rodents marched into my office. That's when I knew: This was no joke.

First came my sister, Thea; then my cousin

Trap; my little nephew Benjamin; the village shaman, Bluster Conjurat; and his daughter, Clarissa. (She is such a **lovely** rodent! I must admit that I have a crush on her.)

Then came my **DETECTIVE** friend, Hercule Poirat; the village chief, Ernest Heftymouse; and finally, Sally Rockmousen!

"Petrified cheese, what is this?" I cried out.

They all stared at me with eyes as hard as **GRANITE**. Did they really think I was the thief?

"Now, see here —" I began, but Ernest Heftymouse cut me off.

"**SILENCE**, Stiltonoot!" he boomed. "Where were you last night? What did you do? With whom? And why? And most important, why were you not in the square with **ALL** (and I mean **ALL**) of

your honest fellow citizens?"

This was starting to sound like an interrogation. But I hadn't done anything wrong!

"I — I was in bed," I stammered nervously. "I h-had a fever. I went under the covers and slept like a ROCK all night long!"

Ernest threw me a glance SHARPER than aged cheddar.

"Ah, so that's your story," he said. "Can anyone confirm this?"

I swallowed hard.

"No, I was alone. But I was in my cave. You have to believe me!" I cried.

Then Thea approached me. She looked so nervous that my throat went DRY.

"Geronimo, two witnesses saw you last night," she said. "But they didn't see you

snoring in your cave."

"They didn't?" I asked.

She shook her head. "No. They saw you **sneaking** out of Gregory Grunt's house, past the sleeping dinosaur guard, and holding the **Da Fossil Cup**!"

They saw you!

I winced. It was **impossible**! Who would accuse me of such a thing?

I know I was asleep in bed. Could I have been **sleepwalking**? No. I would have woken up cold and wet, not warm and refreshed.

Trap defended me. "There must be some mistake," he said. "Geronimo is a scaredy-mouse, and a clumsy one at that. But he's not a thief!"

"That's right!" agreed Benjamin. "There's

33

no one more HONEST than Uncle Ger."

Hearing them stick up for me really touched me, and I shed a little tear. Maybe my family believed me, but it didn't look like anyone else did.

FOSSILIZED FETA, I WAS UP TO MY NECK IN TROUBLE!

Geronimo, a thief? I don't believe it.

Neither do I!

HERE'S THE PROOF!

In the group standing in front of me, one rodent was smiling, secretly pleased at my misfortune. And that rodent was **SALLY ROCKMOUSEN**!

"All the proof points toward you, my dear Stiltonoot," she crowed. "Therefore, you're the thief!"

Surprisingly, Ernest Heftymouse came to my defense.

"Let's change the tone, please," he said. "Of course Stiltonoot is our number one

You're in a nice mess!

suspect, but he hasn't been found guilty yet."

I felt a flicker of hope.

"But the evidence against you is pretty strong, Geronimo," he said, turning to me. "Last night, two witnesses saw you coming out of Gregory Grunt's house with the priceless cup in your PAWS. And those witnesses were none other than . . . Bluster Conjurat and his daughter, Clarissa!"

Gulp!

Here are the witnesses!

Hmm . . .

GULP! That info hit me like a geyser of SCORCHING steam!

Why would Bluster say such a thing? To say nothing of the **bravest**, most beautiful, and smartest rodent in the city — how could Clarissa also be **against** me?

The shaman began his story.

"Clarissa and I were heading toward Singing Rock Square a little later than we had planned," he began. "Clarissa always takes **so long** to do her fur!"

"And you take just as long combing that **BEARD** of yours," Clarissa shot back.

"When we finally got on the road," Bluster continued, "the town looked **DESERTED**. As we passed by Grunt's cave, we saw someone sneakily **JUMPING** out of a window with a bundle in his paws!"

"Of course! The priceless cup was hidden inside the **BUNDLE**!" Sally interrupted rudely.

I was about to say something, but Clarissa cut me off.

"We didn't see the thief's face," she admitted. "But he wore a **green fur** coat — with the exact same **PATTERN** as your coat, Geronimo! I would recognize it anywhere."

I was stunned. My **green fur** coat?

"B-but I left my coat outside to dry last night," I protested.

"A likely story," snorted Sally. **"Prove it!"**

My heart sank. I couldn't prove it. How could I defend myself?

Then my friend Hercule stepped forward, stroking his WHiSKeRS. "There is something here that doesn't add up," he said thoughtfully. "Geronimo is the most HONEST rodent I know. I'm convinced he's not the REAL culprit."

Ernest frowned. "Can you prove he is innocent?"

"Consider it done!" said Hercule confidently. "We will get to the bottom of this."

He took out his magnifying glass and began to EXAMINE my fur coat strand by strand.

"I will give you until the end of the day," Ernest Heftymouse said. "But if you can't prove Geronimo's innocence by tonight,

40

I'll have to declare him guilty!"

Then he looked me in the eye. "If you're guilty, Geronimo, then just return the cup."

Huh?

"But I keep telling you, I don't have it!" I wailed.

"Then you'll have to **pay back** Grunt with something of equal value," the village chief said. "And everyone knows how valuable the Da Fossil Cup is!"

I sighed. I was glad Hercule was **helping** me, but one day wasn't a lot of time.

What if we couldn't find the REAL THIEF? I couldn't return the cup, because I didn't have it. Then I would be forced to give

Gregory Grunt the only thing I had of value: *The Stone Gazette*! Things looked pretty grim.

If I couldn't be a reporter anymore, it would break my furry little heart!

WE'RE ALL ON YOUR SIDE, GERONIMO!

After giving me one last, **STERN** glare, Ernest left. Bluster, Clarissa, and Sally followed him.

Clarissa looked so **DISAPPOINTED** in me! I couldn't bear it. And Sally gave me a **snooty**, satisfied smile. She loved that I was in trouble! But I could tell that Hercule was annoyed with her.

Pbbbt! Hercule stuck out his tongue

Grrr ...

Hee, hee, hee!

and blew a raspberry at her, making a sound like a snakeskin BALLOON letting out air. Sally stomped out and **SLAMMED** the door behind her.

I turned to Thea, Trap, Benjamin, and Hercule — my **biggest** (and maybe only) supporters.

Humph!

"So what do you think, guys?" I asked.

Thea frowned. "It's a **complicated** case."

"No matter," said

Hercule. "We'll solve it! Right, Geronimo?"

I didn't know what to answer.

"Don't worry, Uncle Geronimo," Benjamin said **sweetly**. "We'll help you."

Trap gave me a hearty **SLAP** on the back.

"Relax, Cousin!" he said. "We're all on your side."

Even though the megalithic* slap took

PREHISTO-NOTE

* A megalith was a huge stone used to build monuments in the Stone Age. So the word *megalithic* is sometimes used as an adjective to mean something really big.

the wind out of me, it was nice to know that my friends and family believed I was innocent.

"There is no time to waste," Hercule said, rubbing his **paws** together eagerly. "We must find a solution to this **MESS**! I suggest we make a visit to **GREGORY GRUNT'S** house."

I was starting to feel a little more confident. My family believed in me. And even though someone framed me, I had the **best** detective in Old Mouse City on the case. Well, he was actually the only detective in the city, and he was a little **CLUMSY**. But I trusted him.

It's really true that your friends and family will **always** be there for you!

I opened the door — and a chickenosaurus egg **whizzed** past my face.

"Great rocky boulders!" I cried.

I should have known! Sally and Gossip Radio had continued spreading the word that I was the one who had stolen the cup. Now the entire city was against me.

GULP!

Before I had a chance to say something to calm the **ANGRY** crowd, a shower of rotten eggs hit me.

SPLAT! SPLOSH! SPLASH! SPLAT!

If we wanted to solve the case, we couldn't hide in my office. There was nothing else to do.

"**RUN!**" I yelled.

YOU'RE A THIEF!

ZIGZAGGING like meteorites, we managed to get through the angry crowd. I was the only one to get hit by the **rotten** chickenosaurus eggs. Yuck! With my fur damp and **stinky**, we finally got to Grunt's cave. He did not look happy to see me.

"**YOU'RE A THIEF!**" he roared through his window.

"Mr. Grunt, please try to stay calm!" Thea pleaded.

Grunt drew back the curtain by a millitail* and **PEEKED** out suspiciously.

"We are here to **CONDUCT AN investigation**!" explained Benjamin.

50

"My supersmart snout will SNIFF out the culprit!" added Hercule.

"Are you going to let us in or not, **coconut head**?" asked Trap.

Grunt finally let us in.

"Please show us where the CUP was the night of the theft," said Hercule.

Now, Gregory Grunt is a mouse of few words. He also has the manners of a CAVE BEAR.

But if you look deep into Grunt's eyes, you will see that there is a good mouse in there.

PREHISTO-NOTE
* The basic unit of measurement for Stone Age rodents is the length of the tail of the village leader. A millitail is the length of a portion of the tail – equal to about an inch.

GRUNT! He grunted, annoyed as he showed us the way. "This way." **GRUNT!**

Hercule took out his magnifying glass and began to examine the pedestal where the precious cup had rested.

"**Ah, yes,**" he muttered. "Very good!"

"Did you find something?" I asked.

Here's the pedestal.

?!

This way . . . Grunt!

"No," Hercule replied.

Drat! What a disappointment!

"The thief must be very clever," Hercule said. "He or she did not leave any CLUES that I can see."

Benjamin frowned. "Not one?"

"So we'll look for a clue that I *can't*

JURASSIC BAT DROPPINGS

INSTRUCTIONS FOR USE:

Spread a little powdered droppings on the area in question. Pinch your snout to avoid the nasty smell. After a few seconds, the powder will reveal traces not visible to the naked eye, such as a pawprint or dinosaur footprint.

see," Hercule said with a chuckle. Then he took his **SECRET** weapon from his coat: a small sack of powdered **Jurassic bat droppings**.

Yes, it's **super-stinky**, but it's the perfect tool for revealing invisible footprints. Hercule dusted the floor and . . .

"*BY THE GREAT ZAP!*" he cried. "Look!"

We all looked to where Hercule was pointing.

There, revealed by the powder, was an **IMPRINT**!

To be more exact, it was the pawprint of a rodent's right foot — a very large one. In fact, it was an **enoRMouse** pawprint! And it was right underneath the pedestal where the priceless cup had rested.

Hercule took out a small **red stone** and traced the pawprint with it.

"Geronimo, now put your **PAW** on it," he said.

"Of course!" exclaimed Thea. "We can see if they match!"

I did as Hercule instructed.

My paw was much smaller than the thief's. With this evidence, every suspicion against me would

Aha!

See?

be dropped. There was no way I could be guilty!

But Hercule was still examining the floor with his magnifying glass. Suddenly, he exclaimed, "PETRIFIED BANANAS! What about these?"

MAGNIFYING GLASS

I bent down to look and saw a bunch of tiny jumping dots moving around on the floor.

Hop! Hop! Hop!

Holey cheese! I recognized them immediately. These were prehistoric baby fleas. And not just ordinary baby fleas . . . they were the children of ZIF and ZAF, the fleas who have lived on my green fur coat for many years.

So it was true. Maybe I hadn't been here, but my coat had. But how? I had taken out my coat and left it out to dry as I **snuggled** under my blankets. Had the coat gotten up and walked away by itself?

WHAT A PALEOZOIC PUZZLE!

"There's only one way to solve this case," Hercule declared.

We all stared at him, holding our breath.

"I don't know what it is yet, but I'll figure it out!"

NOW THAT I THINK ABOUT IT . . .

Petrified provolone!

Why, oh, why, do stressful things happen to me all the time?

"Let's keep searching for the guilty party, then," said Thea.

Trap nodded. "That's right. Less chitchat, more investigating!"

"Wait!" cried Hercule. "I have a mousetastic idea. Let's gather all the rodents of Old Mouse City. We'll make each one try the pawprint to see whose is a match."

"That's a fabumouse idea!" Benjamin agreed.

I had to admit that it was a good idea. But for the plan to work, we needed the village chief to agree. Quick as lightning, Hercule and Trap hurried to squeak with Ernest Heftymouse while I stayed behind with Thea and Benjamin.

Ernest Heftymouse

I didn't want to risk another attack of ROTTEN eggs!

While we waited, Thea and Benjamin gave me a quick recap of the *Cavemouse Idol* competition I had missed. A few mice got to perform before the theft was discovered.

The STENCH BROTHERS was the only comedy act that had gone.

"Too bad they weren't funny at all," Benjamin complained.

My whiskers twitched with curiosity. Not funny? That was STRANGE. They were supposed to be famouse comedians — but we only knew that because that's what they told us.

"STINKY and STANKY Stench never told me where they came from," I said.

"I don't know, either," Thea admitted.

"Probably from very far away," guessed Benjamin.

"Don't ask me." chimed in Gregory Grunt. *Grunt!*

He stroked his chin. "But it does remind me of

I remember . . .

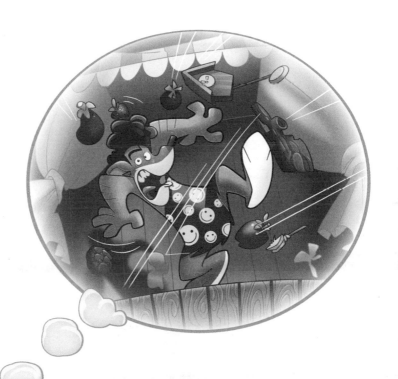

something that happened when I was a **young** rodent."

Grunt said that an **eccentric** rat used to camp out in the streets of the village. He wanted to be called Laffy because he thought he had a great talent for **comedy**. But nobody ever laughed at his jokes.

"They were so bad, the village mice **pummeled** him with vegetables and rotten eggs," Grunt told us. "Finally, Laffy left the city with his newborn triplet sons."

"I don't understand," said Thea. "Do you think Laffy has something to do with the Stench Brothers? But they are **twins**, and Laffy's sons were **triplets**."

"I know," said Grunt. "But there's something else that I just can't quite put my PAW on . . ."

"Please try and think," Thea said.

Grunt nodded.

"Let's see," he said thoughtfully. "Laffy was a terrible comic. He had curly hair, and . . . oh, that's it! He had very large paws! Quite **enoRMouse** paws, in fact. Just like his father, his grandfather, his great-grandfather, and all his ancestors!"

Benjamin's eyes lit up. "Just like the enormouse pawprint left by the **THIEF**!"

"It might just be a coincidence," I said. "After all, the Stench Brothers are twins and Laffy's sons are triplets. It doesn't add up."

"We'll see about that," said Thea, narrowing her eyes **SUSPICIOUSLY**.

Benjamin nodded his head. "Anyway, once

everyone in town tries that **pawprint**, I'm sure we'll find out who really did it. Then you'll be cleared, Uncle Ger."

"But something tells me that the **PAWS** of the Stench Brothers might be just the **RIGHT SIZE**," said Thea.

SATISFIED, STILTONERD?

Suddenly, we heard a **commotion** outside. Hercule and Trap had returned — with all the residents of Old Mouse City behind them! They were there to take the "**pawprint test**."

One by one, they took a turn, each one placing their right paw inside the **enoRMouse** pawprint. The print was too big for everyone! But when there was still a line of rodents to take the test, two of them were trying to *sneak* away.

Fortunately, **Trap** stepped in front of them.

"You're not going anywhere!" he warned.

The two rodents trying to slip away were none other than the Stench Brothers!

"You both have to take the test!" Benjamin told them sternly.

The two rodents shuffled back into the line. To be honest, they were both acting a little strange. They were tense and fidgety, and they were both rubbing their tummies.

"Um, we really can't stay," Stinky said.

"And why not? What are you HIDING?" asked Trap.

"Nothing," said Stanky. "We just ate too many beans at lunch and now —"

"— we really need to use the **prehistoric potty**!" finished Stinky.

"Don't even think about it!" Ernest Heftymouse bellowed. "First, you will take the test!"

So the twins took the **pawprint test** — but

Hee, hee, hee!

Ha, ha, ha!

the result left us squeakless. Yes, the twins did have large paws, **MUCH** larger than all the other rodents. But even those **LarGe PaWS** did not fill the enormouse pawprint!

Hercule, Trap, Benjamin, and I couldn't believe our **EYES**. Thea looked as shocked as if the **GREAT ZAP** had hit her.

There!

"Satisfied, Ms. Stiltonerd?" Stanky said mockingly. "Stil-to-noot! Our last name

is Stiltonoot!" I pointed out in exasperation.

"What did you say, **STILTONOODLE**?" teased Stinky. "Sorry we can't hang around. We have to *run* now."

They scampered away, snickering. There was no hope left for me!

"I'm **doomed**!" I wailed.

Thea didn't seemed bothered by the **bad**

manners of the Stench Brothers. She had a thoughtful look on her face, and I knew she was concentrating harder than ever.

TO JAIL, STILTONOOT!

Rodents kept coming to take the **pawprint test** all day long. But none of the prints fit. Ernest took me by the arm.

Time is running out, Stiltonoot!

"Your time is about up, Stiltonoot!" he said. "If you don't prove your innocence by the time the **SUN SETS**, I'll have to throw you in jail. And you'll have to sell *The Stone Gazette* to get enough shells to pay back Grunt!"

"It's not fair!" I wailed. "My

print doesn't fit. Doesn't that prove I'm **innocent**?"

"We still have our eyewitnesses who **SAW** you at the scene," Ernest reminded me. "And if no other rodent fits that print, then, well . . . maybe you were wearing **BIG BOOTS**."

"I was not!" I protested.

Benjamin held my paw. "Don't give up, Uncle Ger!" he said. But he sounded worried. We were down like **trees struck by lightning**!

Don't give up!

Sigh!

Then a loud voice roused us.

"What's with these long faces, guys? You're giving up? *WE STILTONOOTS NEVER GIVE UP!*"

73

The voice belonged to my sister, Thea. Even though things seemed hopeless, she had a look of true determination stamped on her snout.

"Banish those frowns! Banish those negative thoughts! The time has come for us to make a big move!"

I lifted up my head. Seeing my sister so energetic was like a shot in the arm! Hercule, Trap, and Benjamin felt it as well. I saw Trap crack a hopeful smile.

"Wow, that's what I want to see!" said Thea. "Let's smile like we've got ALL THE CHEESE IN THE WORLD!"

Then she lowered her voice and motioned for us to come closer.

"Listen up: I have a PLAN to catch the thief," she whispered. "But I need all of you for it to work! Without your help, the plan doesn't stand a chance. Are you with me?"

"**YEAHHHHH!**" we all shouted together.

"Marvemouse!" Thea said. "All right, then. All for one, and one for all. **WE'RE GOING ON A MISSION!**"

Hooray!

That's the spirit!

I AM TIGER KHAN!

We **sped** out of Grunt's cave, through the streets of Old Mouse City, until we arrived at the STENCH BROTHERS' wagon.

"But their prints didn't fit," Hercule reminded Thea.

"Quiet!" she hissed. "Unless someone has a better idea, we'll do what I say."

So we FOLLOWED her in silence.

The sun had just set and a blanket of shadows fell over the city.

Holey cheese, I was running out of time!

We hid behind a BUSH in front of the Stench Brothers' wagon. From there we could observe them without being seen.

The COMEDIANS were packing up. It

Shhh!

looked like they were about to **leave** town.

"Listen up," whispered Thea. "Trap is going to imitate the voice of *TIGER KHAN!*"

Let's get going!

?

I jumped. Tiger Khan? What did the **FIERCE** leader of the saber-toothed tigers have to do with this?

"What do you have in mind, **THEA**?" I asked.

My whiskers trembled in fear at the mere mention of the head of the **SABER-TOOTHED SQUAD** — the number one enemy of cavemice everywhere!

Thea just looked at Trap. "Are you up to it, Cousin?" she asked.

"Of course!" he replied. "You should know by now: Nobody can do imitations better than I can."

Then he placed his paws around his mouth. **"STENCH BROTHERS!"** he yelled in Tiger Khan's gravelly voice.

"I AM TIGER KHAN, THE MIGHTY LEADER OF THE SABER-TOOTHED SQUAD!"

Wow, was he good!

79

The brothers **froze**, paralyzed by fear. Thea whispered something in Trap's ear. Trap puffed out his chest and continued shouting in Tiger Khan's voice:

"LISTEN UP, YOU ROTTEN, ROCK-BRAINED RODENTS!"

The twins looked at each other, terrorized. Trap winked at Thea and continued:

"I KNOW THE PRICELESS CUP IS IN YOUR POSSESSION. HAND IT TO ME IMMEDIATELY OR I'LL EAT YOU BOTH FOR MY DINNER!"

H-help!

Trap stopped to catch his breath for a second, and Stinky and Stanky RACED into the wagon faster than if they were being chased by a **T. REX**. They barricaded themselves inside.

I was so proud of my cousin. Trap was more than awesome!

Even Thea seemed totally satisfied.

"Let's see now if the plan worked," she

said **CONFIDENTLY**.

So we stayed hidden, crouched behind the bushes as we waited for a sign from inside the *STENCH BROTHERS'* wagon.

I KNEW IT! I KNEW IT! I KNEW IT!

After what seemed like eons had passed, the DOOR of the wagon finally creaked open.

Creeeeaaaaaaaak!

Stinky was the first one to come out, with his head down and ears drooping. He trembled with fear and looked around with chattering teeth, convinced that Tiger Khan would pounce on him at any moment.

A second later, Stanky, the other twin, PEEKED out. He looked around nervously before he stepped out.

We held our breath. Did Stanky have the stolen cup? But his PAWS were

empty — just like his brother's.

Then something totally **unexpected** happened. The door creaked open again . . . and a **THIRD** rodent stepped out of the wagon!

Our **EYES** widened in amazement. The rodent following the Stench Brothers was identical to Stinky and Stanky, with one difference: His paws were **MUCH,**

MUCH bigger than theirs. In fact, they were enormouse!

So that meant that the Stench Brothers weren't **twins** . . . they were **triplets**!

But the surprises still weren't over. A **fourth** rodent came out of the wagon!

The last mouse was much **older** than the other three, and he also looked like them.

But more interesting than that — he was holding the **STOLEN CUP**!

Thea whispered something in Trap's ear and he started imitating Tiger Khan again.

"AND WHO MIGHT YOU BE?"

Terrified, the rodent immediately put down the cup.

"M-Mr. TIGER KHAN . . . g-grand ruler . . . mighty fanged leader . . . I am the misunderstood comedian, **Laffy**. Please, take the cup and let us go. I beg you!"

At this point, Thea couldn't control herself anymore. She hopped out of the bushes with a jump worthy of a **kangaroosaurus**.

"Aha! You're trapped, you no-good thieves!"

I knew it! I knew it! I knew it!

The rest of us came out of the bushes and found ourselves face-to-face with the Stench family. They **GAPED** at us with their mouths open.

"What's the matter? You're not *laughing* anymore," Thea said, egging them on.

"B-b-but where's Tiger Khan?" asked Stinky, confused.

"**HERE HE IS, YOU GRANITE HEADS!**" Trap growled, imitating the fierce feline once more.

Laffy shook his head of white fur, dejected.

"We've been found with our **paws on the prize**, sons!" he moaned. "Caught in the act like amateurs!"

"How did you **FIGURE It Out**, Thea?" Hercule asked.

"It was Gregory Grunt's story," she said.

"He said Laffy wasn't **funny**, and the Stench Brothers weren't **funny**, either. And where there are twins, there could also be a triplet. So I thought they might be Laffy's sons."

"And you were right!" I said. Then I quickly picked up the cup so I could bring it back to Gregory Grunt.

Whew! what a relief!

A FOOLPROOF PLAN?

By the time we arrived at the village chief's cave, the discovery of the **THIEVES** had spread by word of mouth like **WILDFIRE**. Ernest Heftymouse marched up to the Stench family, who had followed us.

"You should be ashamed of yourselves," he scolded **ANGRILY**. "Out with the **truth**, or we'll ship you straight to the Saber-Toothed Squad!"

Laffy looked embarrassed. He let out a deep sigh.

"Very well! I'll tell

you everything," he began. "My three sons and I came to *Old Mouse City* to teach this town a lesson. Years ago, this same village rejected my comic talent and forced me to leave, showered with boos and rotten eggs."

The old rodent's voice **CRACKED** as he said this. I had a hard time holding back tears. True, he was a thief, but I understood what it was like to be pelted with rotten eggs.

There, there . . .

PAT
PAT

"There, there," I said. "If nobody liked your jokes, maybe you could have . . . ahem . . . changed your PROfeSSion."

Laffy looked at me with tear-filled eyes that broke my **heart**.

"Yes, I know," he said sadly. "But I've always *dreamed* of becoming a great comedian. It's not easy to give up on your dreams."

I could see that Benjamin and Hercule were tearing up as well.

"I thought that stealing the cup would settle the score with this town," Laffy continued. "Instead, now I feel **worse** than before!"

The angry look left Ernest's face.

"Admitting to one's mistakes is **important**," he said solemnly. "Tell me how you stole the cup and pinned the

THE COMPLETE STENCH FAMILY!

FIRST TRIPLET
NAME: STINKY
PROFESSION: STAND-UP COMIC

PROMINENT FEATURE: VERY LARGE PAWS ......

SECOND TRIPLET
NAME: STANKY
PROFESSION: STAND-UP COMIC

PROMINENT FEATURE: VERY LARGE PAWS ......

THIRD TRIPLET
NAME: STUNKY
PROFESSION: STAND-UP COMIC

PROMINENT FEATURE: ENORMOUSE PAWS

FATHER
NAME: LAFFY
PROFESSION: MISUNDERSTOOD COMIC

PROMINENT FEATURE: VERY LARGE PAWS ......

CRIME on Geronimo Stilton."

Stinky Stench stepped forward.

"First of all, we had everyone believe that there were only two STENCH BROTHERS," he said. "But we are triplets. Our third brother, Stunky, was out of sight in the wagon with our father."

"AHA!" I cried. "That's why you wouldn't let me in when I came to interview you."

Laffy nodded. "Correct. We were looking for someone to pin the crime on. And then, when we saw you had a cold and got drenched by the bucket, we knew that you would be spending the night in bed."

I frowned. "So you took advantage of my misery and framed me for the theft. Very clever — but not very nice."

Then Stinky explained the rest of the plan, step-by-step:

1. FIRST, the twins followed me home to make sure my **COLD** knocked me out.

2. THEN, when everyone else was at the show, Stunky (the third triplet) **snuck** out of the wagon and took my **green fur** coat, which I had hung up outside.

3. NEXT, Stunky went **immediately** to Grunt's cave. He got past the sleeping dinosaur without waking it, and stole the priceless cup. While he was there, a few little **fleas**,

Zif and Zaf's children, fell off my coat.

4. THEN, holding the priceless cup, Stunky hightailed it out the **WINDOW**.

It was then that Bluster and Clarissa passed by the cave, saw a mouse in the distance wearing my fur coat, and **ASSUMED** that I was the thief! But I was sound asleep in my **comfy** bed without suspecting a thing.

5. FINALLY, Stunky hid the cup in the Stench Brothers' wagon. Then he put my coat back outside my cave without me knowing.

It was a truly brilliant plot! Nobody in Old Mouse City could have proven my innocence, because everyone was at the talent show. And using my fur coat placed me at the scene of the crime.

Petrified cheese, it was a foolproof plan!

Foolproof, maybe — but not Thea-proof. Or Hercule-proof, either. He had found the enormouse **PAWPRINT**. And Thea's instincts had told her that the Stench Brothers were up to no good. Thanks to those two . . .

THE CASE WAS SOLVED!

THE PROOF OF TRUTH

There was only one thing left to do: Tell everyone that I, Geronimo Stiltonoot, was an HONEST AND INNOCENT cavemouse! Ernest gathered the residents in front of Grunt's cave and told them the truth. Laffy and the triplets, red with **shame**, confessed their guilt and apologized to everyone.

I was so happy, I felt like cheering!

Benjamin hugged me. "Well done, Uncle Geronimo.

Hooray!

I knew you were **NOT** the thief."

Then the rodents of Old Mouse City burst into applause.

CLAP CLAP CLAP!
"HOORAY FOR GERONIMO!"
"Three cheers for Stiltonoot!"

Sally Rockmousen was green with ANGER. "I still think Geronimo is the thief. That enormouse pawprint was just to **distract** us. What rodent could have such a huge 🐾🐾🐾? No one!"

Stunky stepped forward. **"Enough!"** he cried. "I can't allow Geronimo Stiltonoot to be accused anymore."

Then he lifted up his **enormouse** paw in front of the stunned crowd.

See?

99

Sally fumed. *Grunt!*

"Oh, no you don't!" Gregory Grunt spoke up, to everyone's surprise. "I'm the one who says '**GRUNT**'! And I say that Gossip Radio should make an announcement that Geronimo is innocent! Report the truth for once."

"Grunt is right," agreed Ernest. "Go and set the news straight, Sally. **That's an order!**"

Sally was angry, but she couldn't defy the will of the village chief. I finally sighed with relief. I would not have to give up *The Stone Gazette*. **HOORAY!** I felt as light as a prehistoric parrot feather.

I gave a big hug to everyone who had helped. I noticed that Hercule seemed sad.

Humph!

"I'm a prehistoric **failure!**" he declared. "Thea solved the case when I couldn't. I'm an **embarrassment** to detectives everywhere, even though I'm the only one."

"What are you talking about, Hercule?" I asked him. "You made an important discovery that opened up the whole case. If you hadn't seen the **HUGE PAWPRINT**, this case would still be unsolved."

My friend was immediately relieved.

"Actually . . . now that I think about it . . . you're right!" he said happily. "The print was the key to everything. I knew I was the best!"

He strode around the crowd, his chest **puffed out** with pride. "I have a mind as **SHARP** as cheddar cheese! A mind as **fast** as an unlucky rat running from a saber-toothed cat. I am —"

He couldn't finish his sentence, because just then he slipped on a **BANANA PEEL**. He lost his balance, waved his arms **wildly**, spun around, and then **FELL** flat on his snout!

I was about to **BURST** out laughing when somebody beat me to it. You will never guess who it was.

"HO, HO, HO! GrUNt! Ha, Ha, Ha, Ha, Ha!"

That's right! It was none other than Gregory Grunt, who had never **laughed** in his life. He was so used to grunting, though, that he even grunted when he laughed. How funny!

After that I had to thank Thea for trusting her intuition, and for not giving up on me.

"It was a pleasure," she said. "And remember, the next time you're in trouble, keep **FIGHTING** until the bitter end!"

Then, of course, there was Trap and his brilliant acting job.

"AAARGH! I AM GOING TO DEVOUR ALL OF YOU!"

he growled in Tiger Khan's voice, showing off. Then he slapped me on the back, hard.

"Aren't I good?" he bragged. "I'm a born impersonator!"

Trap's words made me think of something **important** — something that couldn't wait anymore. I had to say something to the village chief. . . .

THE CHAMPION OF COMEDY!

"Ernest!" I said, in such a firm tone that everyone instantly fell silent. "There's something very important I want to ask you. **Laffy** and the *STENCH TRIPLETS* realize they've made a mistake. I think they deserve a second chance!"

Laffy and his sons **LOOKED** at me, teary-cyed.

"We are very **sorry** for what we've done," Laffy said. "From the bottom of our **furry** hearts."

Ernest looked at them sternly. "Being **sorry** is not enough," he said. "What are you going to do to redeem yourselves?"

"Well, we were thinking about that," Laffy said. "We would like to use our comic talent to bring cheer to mice who need it."

"We could visit rodents who are elderly or sick," added Stinky.

"Good idea," Ernest said. "But first, we need to continue what you four interrupted.

The **CAVEMOUSE IDOL** contest is back on tonight! We will choose a winner and award the **CUP**!"

"Well, actually . . . ," Gregory Grunt pointed out, "as far as I'm concerned, we already have a winner. **Hercule Poirat, the Champion of Comedy!**"

"Who, me?" Hercule asked, surprised.

"Of course! You made me laugh," said Gregory. "But we can still see the rest of the acts, just for fun."

We all headed to the square. Bluster and Clarissa found me and apologized for believing I was the thief.

Comedy champion?

Are you okay?

I'm great!

Clarissa even gave me a **kiss** on the cheek. "Sorry, Geronimo," she said, and then walked away.

I must admit that Clarissa's kiss made me feel a little bit dizzy. Wiley came to my aid.

"Are you okay, boss?" he asked.

"I'm better than okay . . . I'm **great**!" I replied. "And don't call me boss!"

And then, finally, we all got to see the talent show. I didn't miss it this time! The Stench Brothers performed, and they weren't so bad after all. I actually laughed at

their act. I give you my word on that, or I'm
not . . .

Geronimo Stiltonoot,
cavemouse!

Don't miss any adventures of the cavemice!

#1 The Stone of Fire

#2 Watch Your Tail!

#3 Help, I'm in Hot Lava!

#4 The Fast and the Frozen

#5 The Great Mouse Race

#6 Don't Wake the Dinosaur!

#7 I'm a Scaredy-Mouse!

Up Next!

MEET
GERONIMO STILTONIX

He is a spacemouse — the Geronimo Stilton of a parallel universe! He is captain of the spaceship *MouseStar 1*. While flying through the cosmos, he visits distant planets and meets crazy aliens. His adventures are out of this world!

#1 Alien Escape

#2 You're Mine, Captain!

#3 Ice Planet Adventure

#4 The Galactic Goal

Be sure to read all my fabumouse adventures!

#1 Lost Treasure of the Emerald Eye

#2 The Curse of the Cheese Pyramid

#3 Cat and Mouse in a Haunted House

#4 I'm Too Fond of My Fur!

#5 Four Mice Deep in the Jungle

#6 Paws Off, Cheddarface!

#7 Red Pizzas for a Blue Count

#8 Attack of the Bandit Cats

#9 A Fabumouse Vacation for Geronimo

#10 All Because of a Cup of Coffee

#11 It's Halloween, You 'Fraidy Mouse!

#12 Merry Christmas, Geronimo!

#13 The Phantom of the Subway

#14 The Temple of the Ruby of Fire

#15 The Mona Mousa Code

#16 A Cheese-Colored Camper

#17 Watch Your Whiskers, Stilton!

#18 Shipwreck on the Pirate Islands

#19 My Name Is Stilton, Geronimo Stilton

#20 Surf's Up, Geronimo!

#21 The Wild, Wild West

#22 The Secret of Cacklefur Castle

A Christmas Tale

#23 Valentine's Day Disaster

#24 Field Trip to Niagara Falls

#25 The Search for Sunken Treasure

#26 The Mummy with No Name

#27 The Christmas Toy Factory

#28 Wedding Crasher

#29 Down and Out Down Under

#30 The Mouse Island Marathon

#31 The Mysterious Cheese Thief

Christmas Catastrophe

#32 Valley of the Giant Skeletons

#33 Geronimo and the Gold Medal Mystery

#34 Geronimo Stilton, Secret Agent

#35 A Very Merry Christmas

#36 Geronimo's Valentine

#37 The Race Across America

#38 A Fabumouse School Adventure

#39 Singing Sensation

#40 The Karate Mouse

#41 Mighty Mount Kilimanjaro

#42 The Peculiar Pumpkin Thief

#43 I'm Not a Supermouse!

#44 The Giant Diamond Robbery

#45 Save the White Whale!

#46 The Haunted Castle

#47 Run for the Hills, Geronimo!

#48 The Mystery in Venice

#49 The Way of the Samurai

#50 This Hotel Is Haunted!

#51 The Enormouse Pearl Heist

#52 Mouse in Space!

#53 Rumble in the Jungle

#54 Get into Gear, Stilton!

#55 The Golden Statue Plot

#56 Flight of the Red Bandit

The Hunt for the Golden Book

#57 The Stinky Cheese Vacation

#58 The Super Chef Contest

#59 Welcome to Moldy Manor

Don't miss my journey through time!

Old Mouse City
(MOUSE ISLAND)

GOSSIP RADIO

THE CAVE OF MEMORIES

THE STONE GAZETTE

TRAP'S HOUSE

THE ROTTEN TOOTH TAVERN

LIBERTY ROCK

UGH UGH CABIN

DINO RIVER